WITHDRAWN

MY HOME IS A BATTLEFIELD

J.M. Klein

An imprint of Enslow Publishing

WEST **44** BOOKS™

The TOTALLY SECRET DIARY of DANI D.

New School, New Me!

My Home Is a Battlefield

Star of the Show

Best Friends For-Never

Please visit our website, www.west44books.com.
For a free color catalog of all our high-quality books,
call toll free 1-800-542-2595 or fax 1-877-542-2596.

Cataloging-in-Publication Data

Names: Klein, J.M.
Title: My home Is a battlefield / J.M. Klein.
Description: New York : West 44, 2019. | Series: The totally secret diary of Dani D.
Identifiers: ISBN 9781538381977 (pbk.) | ISBN 9781538381984 (library bound) | ISBN 9781538382998 (ebook)
Subjects: LCSH: Schools--Juvenile fiction. | Self-confidence in children-- Juvenile fiction. | Diaries--Juvenile fiction. | Friendship--Juvenile fiction.
Classification: LCC PZ7.K545 My 2019 | DDC [E]--dc23

First Edition

Published in 2019 by
Enslow Publishing LLC
101 West 23rd Street, Suite #240
New York, NY 10011

Editor: Theresa Emminizer
Designer: Seth Hughes

Photo credits: cover (camouflage pattern) cosveta/iStock/Thinkstock.

Printed in the United States of America

CPSIA compliance information: Batch #CS18W44: For further information contact
Enslow Publishing LLC, New York, New York at 1-800-542-2595.

The TOTALLY SECRET DIARY of

DANI D.

This diary belongs to...

Dani Donaldson
(Don't call me Danielle!)

Age 11

Favorite Foods
Extra chocolaty brownies and PIZZA!

Favorite Color
Purple

Favorite Animal
Horses

Likes
Making extra chocolaty brownies with Dad. Writing in my diary. Movie nights. Making crafts. Watching *Dance For It!* on TV. DANCING!!!

Tuesday, January 8

Grandma keeps telling me to be quiet.

"Dani," she called up the stairs just now. "Can you please turn your music down? Your grandpa is watching his show."

She *always* thinks I'm too loud. But I'm NOT. Not *really*. I just like to dance in my room. That was no problem in my old room in my old house. But now that Mom and I live with Grandma and Grandpa, it is a PROBLEM.

So I put on my new headphones. Mom just bought them for me. She thought that would solve the noise problem. I danced wearing my headphones instead of playing music out loud. But Grandma STILL knocked on my bedroom door.

"You're making the ceiling shake, Dani," she said. "Can you please stop dancing? Don't you have homework?"

I finished my homework already. That's why I was dancing.

Grandma didn't care. She wanted to make dinner without the ceiling shaking. I asked if I could dance after dinner. But she said that's when Grandpa likes to read.

I can't win.

Now I'm writing in my diary instead of dancing. I like to write in my diary. That part is okay. But I also like to dance. I don't like to sit still all day long. I have to sit still in school. I have to sit still to do homework.

Sometimes, I just want to move around.

Mom says it's just for a little bit. I have to be "flexible." That really means she wants me to just do whatever Grandma wants without complaining.

But it's not fair. My mom and dad are "taking a break." Mom and I have lived with Grandma and Grandpa for two whole months. We moved away from my old town. I go to a new school now. In school, I have to share my name with Danny M. I go by "Dani D." now. Danny M. is the most annoying boy EVER. My old friends are far away. My dad is far away.

And now Grandma wants me to be quiet.

I think Grandma and I need to take a "break."

Here is everything I can't do at Grandma's house:

• Make extra chocolaty brownies in the kitchen. Dad and I used to make extra chocolaty brownies all the time. But Grandma always says "no" when I ask to make them here. Mom can't cook here, either. Mom likes to cook. But

Grandma doesn't like it when anyone else uses her stove. This makes Mom sad.

• Watch *Dance For It!* Grandma says I can't watch TV at night. The only TV is in the living room. That's where Grandpa likes to read. Now I don't know who gets voted off until WAY after everyone else! I watch clips on my phone. But that is NOT THE SAME. I already know who is going home!

• Hang out with other kids. I can't have anyone from school over. And there are no kids in Grandma's neighborhood. Only old people live here.

Maybe it's a good thing I am writing in my diary now instead of dancing. Now I see that Mom and I should not live here anymore. There is only one way to solve this problem.

Mom and Dad need to get back together.

Thursday, January 10

I have a BIG problem.

I've been hoping Mom and Dad would get back together soon. This was supposed to be just a break. But something REALLY bad just happened.

Mom started a new job today. And she got asked out on a date!

A DATE!!!!

I've seen the guy who asked her out. He works with Mom now. But he also lives on Grandma's street. He has hair IN HIS EARS. And Mom said yes! She said yes to the ear-hair guy!

EWWWWWWWWWWWW!!!!

I don't know what Mom is thinking. I know she is sad when Grandma doesn't let her cook. But Ear-Hair Guy is not going to make her happy. That's for sure.

Mom obviously
needs my help.
She doesn't even
realize she is making
a bad decision.

I told her that. I said,
"Mom, why would you date
someone who has hair in
their ears?"

And Mom told me to "be nice." I was being
nice! I was being nice to *her*. Imagine kissing
someone with ear hair!

EWWWWW!

But Mom said, "It doesn't matter whether
someone has hair in their ears, Dani. That's not
what is important in life."

Well. She was right about that. What's
important in life is moving home. Back with Dad
and my best friend Emily Grace and my old
room and all my other friends.

So I asked Mom when we are moving home.

Mom frowned and said, "Dani, we live here now."

And then she started talking about her new job!

This is not good. Mom's new job means she is not thinking about going home. It means she is thinking of staying here. Forever. I don't want to live here forever! I don't even want to live in Grandma's house NOW.

I miss my dad. I don't understand why Mom doesn't miss Dad, too.

Mom is happy about her new job. I want her to be happy. But I also want to go home. I thought we were just going to live here for Mom and Dad's "break." Then they would get back together, and we could go home.

Now it's up to ME. I have to be the one to fix this. Mom and Dad need to get back together.

And I'm going to make it happen.

Saturday, January 12

It's easy to decide you are going to do something.

It's much harder to actually do it.

All last week, I tried thinking of ways to get Mom and Dad back together. At first, I couldn't think of anything. At all. Which was bad because Mom went on ANOTHER date with Ear-Hair Guy.

I was stuck at home with Grandma and Grandpa while Mom went out. Grandma wanted to teach me how to knit.

"Knitting is a good way to sit still, Dani," she said.

I decided to video chat Dad instead. Dad and I video chat all the time. It helps, but I still miss him tons.

Dad is usually pretty funny and makes me laugh. But tonight, he seemed a little sad. I asked him what was wrong.

"Oh, nothing big," Dad said. "I just had a bad day at work. That's all."

Dad's face didn't *look* like he was lying. But still. Dad loves his job. I don't see how work would have made him sad. I think he's sad because he misses Mom and me. He just didn't want to tell me.

So I told Dad all about how much I love him and how proud I am of him. And that seemed like it cheered him up. He at least smiled a little bit.

It gave me an idea.

"Mom's been asking about you," I said.

Dad sat up straighter. "Really?" he asked. "She has?"

I nodded. "She asks about you *all the time*."

"Oh," he said. "I...I didn't know that."

Here is the truth: Mom NEVER asks about Dad.

"What has Mom been asking?" Dad asked.

"Oh, she asks how you're feeling. Or what you're doing. Mom cries a lot now. She's really sad. She says she misses you a lot."

"She misses me?" Dad asked. "Really?"

Here is the truth: Mom never cries. She also doesn't say she misses Dad a lot. But obviously she DOES miss Dad. She just doesn't tell me. And she can't be happy if she is dating Ear-Hair Guy.

So it's not *really* a lie.

"Yes, really," I said. "She *really* misses you."

Dad got quiet after I told him how much Mom missed him. It was like he couldn't stop thinking about it. He didn't talk anymore about work, that's for sure. That MUST mean he misses Mom, too.

So I have a plan now.

I'm going to help Mom and Dad. If they can't tell each other how they feel, I will do it for them. I will make sure they KNOW how much they miss each other—by telling them myself. They SHOULD miss each other. I miss us all together. So if I say it enough—it will be true. If I say it enough—they will get back together.

This is going to be my BIGGEST *total secret* ever. And it's going to have to stay that way.

Monday, January 14

I'm writing this in school.

I can't write at home now because I don't want Mom to find my diary. Or worse—Grandma. All of this is a TOTAL SECRET.

Last night, I told Mom how much Dad misses her. And she was ALSO surprised. She ALSO wanted to hear more about how much he missed her.

I added a few details.

They weren't all *really* true. But my English teacher, Mrs. Kim, says a good story has good details.

So I told Mom some good details. I told her Dad was so sad, his face was pale. I told her Dad missed her so much, he asked a million questions about her. I told her Dad said he loved her more than anything.

"Dad said you were the best thing in his life,"

I said. "He said you were his sunshine and his moon."

That last part may have been a bit *too* much. Grandma laughed when she heard it. But Mom kept thinking about it. I could tell.

And then the best thing happened.

Mom called Dad.

On the phone! The actual phone!

Mom and Dad never talk now. This is all part of their "break." They've talked ONCE since we moved. And that was about me. I can't remember the last time they really talked, just the two of them.

But Mom called Dad last night.

Clearly, my plan is working.

Mom and Dad are SO going to get back together. They will realize I am right. They will realize they DO miss each other. They will realize we should be a family again.

Ugh. Danny M. keeps trying to read my diary. He sits next to me in Mrs. Kim's class. He is so ANNOYING. Doesn't he know this is a TOTAL SECRET?!

I KNOW YOU CAN SEE THIS, DANNY M. STOP READING MY DIARY NOW!!

Thursday, January 17

My plan worked!!!!!!

Dad is coming for a visit!!!!!! He's going to stay with us. He's going to see my new room. And he's going to see my new school. He will actually pick me up from school tomorrow! I get to see him before everybody!

And then I KNOW he and Mom will get back together.

Yes!!

I'm so glad I did this. Mom and Dad have been talking on the phone much more now. This is such a good sign. I even have school off on Monday. So we will have LOTS of time together.

Everything is going to work out.

I just know it.

Friday, January 18

My dad is so fun.

We are at my grandparents' house now. But no one else is here. It's just us. And we are making extra chocolaty brownies together.

I've missed extra chocolaty brownies so much!

My dad makes the best brownies. They are so gooey and yummy. The brownies are in the oven now. It's so hard to wait for them to be done. So I'm writing at the kitchen table to distract myself. The brownies smell AMAZING. Like all the extra chocolate in the world!

I wish I could eat them every day.

Maybe now I can!

Dad picked me up from school. I was so excited to see him. He was waiting out front for me—and I JUMPED right into his arms.

Danny M. saw me jump. He laughed. But my dad is a police officer. He gave Danny his most serious police officer look. And Danny M. just hurried away.

It was so funny.

I told Dad all about how ANNOYING Danny M. is. How he made fun of me when I first started school. How we share a nickname. How he sometimes teases me. How he waits until I get to math class. And then starts talking to Leo Thomson REALLY loudly. Just so I know he's ignoring me.

And then the whole way back to Grandma's, Dad and I made fun of Danny M.

Mom would have just said to be nice. But Dad really listens. I'm SO happy he's here.

"What do you want to do first, Dani?" Dad asked. "What do you miss most?"

I thought for a while.

And then I said, "Extra chocolaty brownies!"

Dad laughed. "We should make them!"

"But Grandma doesn't let me bake in her kitchen," I told him. "She likes her kitchen to be really clean."

"Well, *I* am here with you," Dad says. "And *I* say it's okay. I'm your dad, and I give you permission. We'll clean up the kitchen after we're done."

That made sense to me.

The brownies are almost done! We tried the batter. It tasted even better than I remembered. I can't wait until Mom gets home. I bet she will jump into Dad's arms, too. Or if she doesn't—wait until she tastes these brownies!

Everything is going to go back to how it was before. Everything is going to be wonderful.

Oh!! Mom's home now!!!

Friday, January 18

Extra chocolaty brownies almost ruined everything!

That was NOT how it was supposed to go. Normally, extra chocolaty brownies make everything better. But instead it was almost a COMPLETE DISASTER.

It's all Grandma's fault.

If Mom had been by herself, everything would have been fine. I bet we would be in Dad's car now. We would be driving home. I might have even seen Emily Grace tomorrow.

But no.

That's not happening.

Because Grandma came home with Mom.

Grandma took one look at the kitchen. She saw melted chocolate on the counters. She saw chocolate on the floor. She saw chocolate on her stove.

She FLIPPED OUT.

And man, then the yelling started.

Not even from Grandma. From Mom and Dad!

Mom didn't even yell at me. She yelled at DAD!

She saw Grandma's face. And then she yelled, "Mike, what are you doing? Look at this mess!"

And then Dad got upset and said, "Calm down, Kelly. I was going to clean it up. You always jump in on me. You always assume the worst."

Whenever my parents start calling each other by their actual names, I know it's going to be BAD.

It was.

"I always assume the worst?!" Mom yelled. "This is just like you, Mike. You always do whatever you want. This is not your kitchen. You know how my mother is. You know she likes her kitchen clean. And then you just come in and do whatever you want anyway!"

Dad yelled back. And Mom yelled again. They shot back and forth with mean comments. It's like my home is a battlefield!

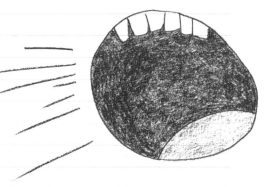

Thank goodness the oven timer went off. They probably would have kept yelling forever. But Dad had to stop fighting to get the brownies out of the oven. Mom at least calmed down a little when she saw the brownies. So at least chocolate still does *something*.

Grandpa came home then. He got Grandma out of the house. And then Mom and Dad and I cleaned the kitchen up. Nobody talked. But at least nobody yelled.

The kitchen is all clean now. But Mom and Dad still aren't talking. Mom is upstairs in her room by herself. Dad is texting. How are they going to get back together if they aren't even talking?!

I have to fix this NOW!

Friday

I came up with a better plan. And THIS time, I KNOW it's going to work.

I went and found Mom. I told her it was all my idea to make extra chocolaty brownies. (It was.) I said I was really, really sorry for causing so much trouble. (I was.)

I said, "Dad was really excited to see you. He couldn't stop talking about you. He kept saying how much he missed you."

Dad hadn't *exactly* said those things. But that's only because we were so busy making brownies. He just hadn't said them *yet*. I know he is *going* to say them sometime. So those also weren't really lies.

Mom finally came down. She told Dad she was sorry. "Thanks for spending time with Dani today," she said to Dad. This time she didn't use his first name. "I know she missed making those brownies."

And Dad smiled. "I'm glad we got to do it. I really am sorry for the mess."

Thank goodness! Everything was working out! Finally!

I gave both Mom and Dad a hug. I told them it meant SO much to me that we were all together.

"Maybe we could do something together tomorrow?" I asked. "As a family?"

So now we are going to the zoo tomorrow!

Mom tried to get us to go shopping. Dad wanted to go ice-skating. But I said I REALLY REALLY wanted to go to the zoo. I said I was the only kid at my school who hasn't been to the zoo. That it was embarrassing.

That's not really true.

I have no idea who has been to the zoo. No one talks about going to the zoo with their parents. No one talks about doing anything with their parents!

The zoo is where Mom and Dad went on their very first date. They had their first kiss in front of the elephants.

They haven't talked about it for a long time. But I still remember it. They used to give each other elephants ALL THE TIME. Stuffed elephants. Glass elephants. Polka-dotted elephants. If they saw an elephant, they bought it for each other.

So I just have to get them to the elephants tomorrow. They have to see the elephants. THEN they will remember how much they love each other.

This is a MUCH better idea. I should have thought of it first. Of course Mom and Dad shouldn't see each other for the first time around Grandma! They won't be around my grandparents tomorrow. It will be MUCH better. The zoo here is supposed to be pretty good, too. We can be a happy family there. It's going to be a fun day.

And Mom and Dad will fall back in love with each other.

I just KNOW it.

Still Friday

Oh, the extra chocolaty brownies were pretty good, actually. Not the best ever. (They were a little overbaked.) But still REALLY GOOD.

Saturday, January 19

I don't understand my parents most of the time.

I REALLY don't understand them today.

We are in the car. We're driving to the zoo. It should be so exciting and fun. It should be laughter and promises of cotton candy.

But no.

Not with MY parents.

My parents are SILENT.

I'm sitting in the back seat writing in my diary. I'm writing because I got so bored. No one has said ONE word in the last FIVE MINUTES.

I guess it's better than it was when we first left.

First, Mom and Dad fought because Dad was late.

Then they fought over who would drive. Mom won. She's driving now.

Then they fought over whether to stop for food. Dad won. We got breakfast sandwiches.

I don't get it. They are fighting over every little thing.

Why can't they just be excited to see the monkeys? Monkeys are cool!

It's going to be okay though. I just have to get them to the elephants.

Saturday

We're at the zoo now. I'm sitting at a picnic table while Dad pays for lunch. Mom's getting ketchup.

Mom and Dad just got into a fight about spending money on bottled water. Dad wanted to buy a bottle. Mom said bottled water was a waste of money.

"Just get a drink out of the water fountain, Mike," Mom said.

Dad got all frowny-faced. "Don't tell me what to do, Kelly! I'm not a child. I'm an adult. I can buy bottled water if I want to."

They haven't even noticed I am writing in my diary. All my TOTAL SECRETS right in front of them. They don't care. They keep

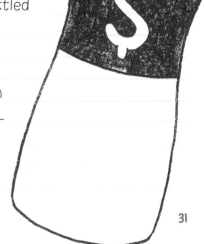

fighting. About EVERYTHING.

This stinks. This fighting is even worse than before. Why can't they just get along?

We haven't seen the elephants yet. I keep trying to get us there. But one of them keeps finding something else we should look at first.

So I'm going to try something else. I brought my Christmas money just in case. After we finish eating, I'm going to ask to look in the gift shop. Mom and Dad hate gift shops. So I know they will let me go by myself. There will be lots and lots of elephants there. I will use my Christmas money to buy Mom an elephant. I will tell her it's from Dad.

Then they can stop all this stupid fighting.

It's getting ANNOYING.

Saturday

I am in the gift shop at the zoo. I have to make this quick. Mom and Dad are outside waiting for me. I'm only writing because I'm not sure what to do.

It's just like I thought. There are a MILLION elephants in the gift shop. Big elephants. Small elephants. Wood elephants. Stuffed elephants. One elephant that is really, really ugly but costs a lot of money.

I have enough of my Christmas money left. But now I'm not sure this is a good idea.

This seems like an *actual* lie. More of an actual lie than the other stuff I've been saying. That stuff I'm just hoping is true. Or pretending is true. But if I give Mom an elephant, I will know for sure it is a lie. I will know for sure Dad didn't give it to her.

It will be an actual, for sure, lie.

But I really, really want Mom and Dad to get

back together. And I REALLY want them to stop fighting.

It is SERIOUSLY ANNOYING. They won't stop!

One elephant seems like a small price to pay. Even if it is an actual, for sure, lie.

I made my decision.

I'm going to buy a *small* elephant. The store has a key chain elephant. It's tiny. It will fit in my pocket. So Mom and Dad won't see it. They won't know I bought it. I can keep it a secret.

BUT! I'm going to try the real elephants first. I'm going to MAKE Mom and Dad go to the elephant area next. If that doesn't work, THEN I will give Mom the key chain. It will be a backup plan only. I won't tell a big lie—unless I have to.

So the elephants have GOT to work.

Saturday

THE ELEPHANTS ARE NOT WORKING!

Both the real elephants and the fake elephant!

I don't know what else to do.

Mom and Dad were supposed to see the elephants and remember they loved each other. But Mom just sighed and checked her watch. And Dad didn't even look up from his phone!

I thought the elephant area would be a little magical. But it's kind of smelly here. And cold. Even the elephants look a little sad. Their trunks are all droopy, and they aren't really doing anything. It's kind of a WEIRD place for a first kiss. In the movies, the first kiss is always in a field of flowers. Or in front of a castle. But that's my parents. Weird about EVERYTHING.

So I did it. I gave Mom the elephant key chain I bought.

I waited until Dad was reading a sign with elephant facts. Then I pretended I wanted Mom to see something closer to the elephants. And I pulled out the key chain.

"This is from Dad," I said. "He wanted me to give it to you."

I didn't like saying it. It FELT like a lie. My stomach felt squishy. And I couldn't even look at Mom's face.

But I knew I had to do it. I had to fix this.

I don't think it worked though. Mom didn't act happy. She frowned. "Why didn't he give it to me himself?"

This was a really good question. I did not have a really good answer.

"Uh, he wanted it to be a surprise," I said. "But isn't it cute? It's like all your other elephants. All the other elephants Dad got you."

I thought maybe Mom needed a reminder. But that didn't work. Mom kept frowning.

"Dad shouldn't be getting you involved," she said. "This is between me and your dad. Not you."

And then she told me to wait on this bench. "Just write in your diary for a moment, Dani," she said. "I want to talk to your dad."

That's what I'm still doing now. Writing in my diary on this bench while Mom talks to Dad.

I don't like that my mom is using my diary to distract me. My diary is MY diary. But I guess I don't mind that she wants to talk to him. Maybe that's a good thing?

I don't know, though. Mom looks MAD. She and Dad are talking in this really INTENSE way. They are all the way on the other side of the elephant area from me. So I can't hear them.

But they are both frowning. And now Dad looks mad, too.

Now everyone near them is giving them funny looks. Or moving away from them.

I'm going to get closer. I'm going to write down what they say. Maybe that will help me figure out stuff later.

Mom is saying, "I thought we agreed we would keep Dani out of our problems, Mike."

"I *am* keeping Dani out of our problems," Dad says. "I don't like your tone, Kelly."

Tone is a big thing to my dad. But my mom ALWAYS gets upset when my dad talks about *tone*. Too bad Dad never asks me what to say. I would tell him that's a bad idea. Because, yup. Mom is getting upset. Her face is all red, and she's breathing hard.

Mom: I don't understand *why* you are acting this way, Mike.

Dad: Why I am acting this way? This whole day, it's been one thing after another. You keep picking fights with me.

Mom: You keep picking fights with me! I don't understand why you are acting this way if you love me and miss me so much.

Dad: I don't understand why you are acting this way if you've been crying over missing me so much.

Mom: What are you talking about? I haven't been crying! Who told you I've been crying?

Uh-oh.

Saturday

Mom and Dad know the truth now.

I'm in BIG trouble.

And Mom and Dad are in the middle of the biggest fight ever. They yelled so loud the zoo people asked them to leave. They said they were bothering the animals!

I'm not sure who I feel sorrier for—me or the elephants.

Actually, that's not true. I would much rather be an elephant right now. An elephant isn't a big liar. An elephant doesn't care if its life is RUINED.

We are in the car now. This is the worst car ride of my ENTIRE LIFE. Neither of them is talking now.

Mom and Dad figured out every single one of my lies. They know I lied that they missed each other. They know I lied about Mom crying. They know I lied that they still love each other. They know I lied when I gave Mom the elephant key chain.

The elephant key chain was the worst lie. Mom gave it back to me. I'm holding it now. It means I can't pretend I didn't lie. They have proof. And I remember what I did every time I look at it.

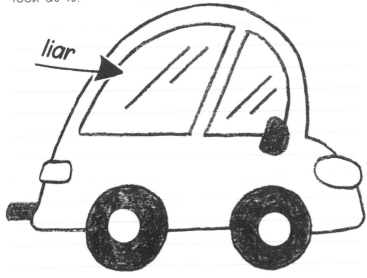

liar

I've never felt this bad.

Never.

Still Saturday

I'm in my room now.

Mom and Dad dropped me off at Grandma and Grandpa's. They said they need to talk now.

I tried to tell Mom how sorry I am. But she said, "Not right now, Dani. This isn't about you."

Only it IS about me. I made everything worse by lying. If I hadn't lied, Mom and Dad would still be on their "break." The "break" was better than this fight. And they wouldn't have had so many little fights. They wouldn't have been confused about why the other person was acting differently.

I don't know what to do.

I ruined everything.

I shouldn't have lied about how my parents felt. They were lies all along. I knew Mom didn't really miss Dad. I knew she was happy. But I think I *wanted* to believe that she missed Dad.

Because *I* missed Dad.

I was the one who wanted everything to go back to the way it was before. Everything I told Mom and Dad that the other person felt—those were things *I* felt.

I should have just told them all that. I should have just told them how I felt instead of lying about how they felt. I know that now.

It's all just so confusing sometimes. Sometimes, you don't really know how you feel. Sometimes, it's hard to explain what you don't know to other people.

But I guess all you can do is try.

I'm going to try now.

I'm going to tell Mom and Dad how I feel as best as I can. As much as I understand.

Maybe if I text them that I'm sorry and want to talk they will come home?

Saturday

Mom and Dad came back.

I told them a lot of stuff.

I sat them down at the kitchen table like it was an important business meeting.

I said I was sorry.

I said I just wanted them back together. I said I was tired of living at Grandma and Grandpa's house.

"I just want to go home," I said. "I miss Dad. I want things back the way they used to be."

Mom and Dad listened to me. They seemed like they understood.

But then they told me their own news.

They are getting divorced.

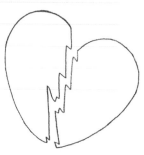

Tuesday, January 22

I don't feel as sad as I thought I would.

I don't LIKE that my parents are getting a divorce. At all. But I like that I know what is going to happen next. I like not worrying. I like not wondering if we'll be together again.

And here's what I REALLY like.

Mom and Dad aren't fighting. They look happier. Happier than I can remember them looking for a long time. Dad doesn't seem so tired. And Mom looks less worried.

I still wish we could all live together. That's the part I'm sad about. And that's what I told Mom and Dad Saturday night.

"I want us all to be a family," I said.

"We still *are* your family," Dad said. "We still love being your parents. Your mom and I are just better apart."

Mom hugged me. "It's okay to be sad and upset," she said. "But we still love you, Dani. Our divorce has nothing to do with you."

I wasn't sure about that. It felt like it was all my fault. Because I had lied. So I told them I was sorry for lying. And then I said I was sorry ten more times.

But they said they weren't mad at me. They said they understood.

They just don't want me to lie again.

"We want you to *talk* to us about your feelings," Mom said. "Especially when you are upset."

"You can tell us anything," Dad said. "We won't get mad at you. We want you to tell us when you are scared. Or when you are afraid. Or when you are lonely and miss the way things used to be. You don't need to keep your feelings a secret, Dani."

That surprised me. I didn't think I kept my

feelings a secret. I thought only my plan was a *total secret*. But I guess I also keep the way I feel a secret, too. I write my feelings down here instead.

I still think writing my feelings down is easier.

But I guess telling my feelings can be nice, too. Like it was fun when I told Dad how ANNOYING Danny M. was.

At school today, Danny M. made a face at me. But I didn't get mad. I remembered how Dad had looked at Danny M. all serious-like. And I laughed. And Danny M. just turned red.

It was so funny.

I really like embarrassing Danny M.

Dad left today. That part felt the worst. I'm going to video chat with him tonight. But I still wish I could see him every day. I think I will always wish that. But Dad said he'll come to visit me here more often. And Mom said I could spend the whole summer with Dad.

AND the best part is—WE ARE MOVING!!!!

Mom and I are, at least.

"I know you've been having a tough time," Mom told me. "I thought it was good for you to be around your grandma and grandpa. But now I think it's better if we get our own place."

So we are getting our own place!!

Now that Mom has a new job, she wants to buy a new house. But for now we are moving into an apartment. I won't have to change schools again. And I can bake in the kitchen as long as Mom is there and I clean up when I am done.

It's going to be SO much better.

Saturday, February 2

It's moving day!

Mom and I moved into our apartment today. It's beautiful. It's not as nice as my old house. It's not as nice as Grandma and Grandpa's place. But I love it so much!

The best part is my new room. It's SO big. I have a big closet. And a big window. It's going to be my new favorite spot to write in my diary.

And I can dance and dance and dance!!

That's the first thing I did. It was before there was even furniture in my room. I ran in. And I turned my music WAY up loud. I didn't even bother to put on my headphones. And I danced and danced and danced.

49

Mom laughed. She said I still couldn't play my music too loud late at night. But I can still dance in my room. AND I can watch *Dance For It!* at night. My favorite dancer is even still there!

Mom and I already baked in the kitchen. But we made chocolate chip cookies. NOT extra chocolaty brownies. I decided I want that to be my thing just with Dad. But the chocolate chip cookies were still pretty good.

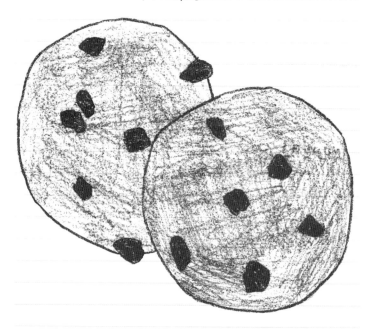

I know my parents are still going to do stupid things. I know they will still get into fights. And I know they will still be annoying. They are parents, after all.

But I know I don't like it when people make decisions for me. I didn't like when Grandma tried to tell me what to do. We get along MUCH better now that we don't live together. Now she can just be my grandma. Like she used to be.

So I decided I'm not going to tell other people what to do. I'm not going to tell my parents they should be together if they don't want to be. I'm going to stay out of it. I still miss all three of us being together. But it's nice when they aren't fighting all the time. It's nice when they can just be my mom or my dad.

I still miss my dad. And I miss Emily Grace and my other friends.

But it can be a home here, too. A new home that's NOT a battlefield. And that makes me want to dance again!

Want to Keep Reading?

Turn the page for a sneak peek
at the next book in the series.

9781538381991

Tuesday, February 5

The Pirate Queen.

That's the name of the new school play. *The. Pirate. Queen.*

Titles are important. They tell you if something is going to be stupid. Or if it's going to be cool. And *The Pirate Queen* tells you SO much. It tells you the play is going to be about an awesome girl. Who is a pirate AND a queen.

A pirate and a queen! A girl who is the boss! I can't imagine anything better than that. And neither can any other girl in my middle school. At school today, that was all anyone could talk about. We got in trouble in science because we weren't paying attention.

"This might be on the test," Mr. Gisi said. I can't remember what he was talking about. "This is very important."

Ha! Like it's more important than *The Pirate Queen!*

Mr. Gisi made us all take notes. He wanted us to "focus." But making us take notes didn't do anything. We still all talked about *The Pirate Queen* at lunch. And in the hallways. And then during math.

"This is going to be so *amazing*," I heard Hailey say. Hailey is usually the star of the school plays. "Mrs. Leonard says we are going to learn how to sword fight!"

Even the boys talked about it. I caught Danny M. talking to Leo and Jayden before English. But they weren't talking about the *interesting* stuff. They didn't talk about the adventures the Pirate Queen leads. Or the sword fights she wins. Or the journey she goes on to save the kingdom. They kept saying "*Arrrr*" and "Ahoy, matey!" over and over again. It was ANNOYING.

I rolled my eyes at Danny M. "You guys are *so* immature," I told him.

He made a face at me. "I bet *you* want to be the Pirate Queen, Dani D.," he said. "Just like all the other girls. Admit it."

I was NOT going to admit it. Not to Danny M., that's for sure. Danny M. is the most annoying boy EVER. Every day he does something to bug me—all because he has to share a first name with me.

But he was right.

EVERY girl wants to be the Pirate Queen.

Including me.

ABOUT THE AUTHOR

J.M. Klein is a former journalist who has lived all around the country and moved half a dozen times. Like Dani, she learned how to make new friends and tried out for the school play. She didn't make that play, but she did develop a lifelong love of theater and now has good friends in many states. She's always written in diaries and journals, the contents of which are still totally secret.

The TOTALLY SECRET DIARY of DANI D.

Check out more books at:

www.west44books.com

An imprint of Enslow Publishing

WEST 44 BOOKS™

Growing Up Groovy
An Out of This World Adventure

Robin Epstein

Scholastic Inc.

New York Toronto London Auckland Sydney
Mexico City New Delhi Hong Kong Buenos Aires

Read all the books about the Groovy Girls!

To Susan B., a fantastic co-pilot who always makes
the journey memorable and the destination better.

Cover illustration by Taia Morley

Interior illustrations by Yancey Labat

ISBN 0-439-81437-5

The Groovy Girls™ books are produced under license from Manhattan Group, LLC.
Go to groovygirls.com for more Groovy Girls fun!

12 11 10 9 8 7 6 5 4 3 2 1   6 7 8 9 10/0

Printed in the U.S.A.
First Little Apple printing, September 2005

Chapter 1

The Schockeroo's On You!

Wait!" Reese said to O'Ryan, as the twins crept toward the big front window of their mom's store, "Hey, Betty," after soccer that afternoon.

Practice had ended a little early, so the girls had decided to make their mom the happy recipient of a "McCloud Sister Shockeroo."

"We want to make sure she doesn't see us before we see her," Reese instructed her seven-minutes-older sister, peeking in to the front of the store.

"I *know*," O'Ryan replied, "but we can't surprise her from way out *here*."

"I see Mom standing by the dressing room in the back of the store," Reese continued. "I'll bet she's helping a customer!"

"Good work, Detective No-Duh," O'Ryan answered. "*Of course* she's helping a customer—what else would she be doing?"

"Maybe we should wait till the shopper leaves," Reese responded.

"Oh, come on," O'Ryan replied. "I'm sure any customer of Mom's would love getting surprised by us, too!"

O'Ryan did have a point.

The people who shopped in their mother's vintage clothing store usually had a groovy sense of humor that matched their love of quirky clothes.

"Okay," said Reese, "so on my count, we'll run in the door and yell 'surprise!'"

"One..."

"Two..."

But just as Reese was about to yell, "Th-rrr-eeee!"

she stopped mid-*rrr*.

The reason?

Well, at that very moment, the girls saw the dressing room curtain open, and they spied an incredible…an unbelievable…a perfectly ridiculous sight.

It was none other than their fourth-grade teacher, Mrs. Pearlman!

But she wasn't looking like the plain-Jane fourth-grade teacher that the girls knew and loved.

No. Not that.

She was looking like a regular glamour girl!

Good old Mrs. P. in an ooh-la-la black satin fringed dress, long gloves ringed with rhinestone bracelets, and T-strap high-heeled patent leather shoes!

O'Ryan's mouth dropped open as her eyes widened to the size of salad plates.

The shock was almost too great to keep the twins from bursting into laughter...almost, but not quite.

Eh-heh-heh-heh-heh-heh!

Ah-ha-ha-ha-ha-ha!

Ee-hee-hee-hee-hee-hee!

SNORT!

"If I didn't see it with my very own eyes," O'Ryan said, doubled over in laughter, "I wouldn't believe it."

"*I know*!" Reese giggled. "And since I *am* seeing it with my very own eyes, I'm wondering if I need glasses!"

"Who'd-a thunk that this is what our teacher looks like when she's not in class?"

"So what now?" Reese replied. "Should we run in and surprise Mom *and* Mrs. P.?"

O'Ryan tapped her finger to her chin and gave it a good think. Then she looked back through the store window and saw Mrs. Pearlman delightedly examining herself in the three-way mirror.

"No way," O'Ryan said, shaking her head. "I mean, just look at her! I bet she'd be totally embarrassed if she knew we'd seen her in that crazy get-up."

Reese looked back through the window and watched as her fourth-grade teacher did a little hip shake, making her dress fringes fly.

"Sister," Reese said, "when you're right—which is not that often—you're right!"

So the girls quickly ducked down and slowly began creeping away from the store window.

It wasn't until they were safely behind a tree and out of sight that O'Ryan turned back.

"Okay," O'Ryan said, "now look, I know you

have trouble keeping things secret. And I'll bet you're just bursting to tell someone what you've just seen. *But,*" she continued, "I think we should make a pinky promise that we keep this to ourselves."

Reese looked at O'Ryan and nodded. "All right," she said, holding her pinky up and extending it to her sister. "It's for the best. After all," Reese said smiling, "if we told anyone that Mrs. Pearlman was really a disco queen outside of school, who would believe us, anyway?!

Chapter 2

Spilling-and Counting- the Beans

"**Y**ou're hiding something," Oki said, staring at O'Ryan, as the two best friends worked on their language arts assignment together later that afternoon.

"No, I'm not," O'Ryan replied, shaking her head and desperately trying to squash the smile that she could feel blossoming on her face.

If she smiled, O'Ryan knew she'd start laughing. And *if* she started laughing, well, then *fahgetaboutit*,

7

she wouldn't be able to hold anything back. O'Ryan had been so itchy to spill Mrs. Pearlman's secret, she'd been doodling pictures of ladies dressed in be-fringed dresses all over her notebook.

"O'Ryan McCloud, first of all, keeping a secret from your best friend is practically a crime in certain states," Oki said. "*And*," she added, narrowing her eyes, "*lying* to that friend about the secret is even worse than wearing matchy-match clothes!"

O'Ryan's eyes darted from side to side. Then she slid off her bed and quietly closed the bedroom door. "Okay," she whispered. "If I tell you, do you promise on the fur of your kitty cat, that you won't tell another soul about this?"

Oki nodded and her eyes widened as she prepared to hear the secret.

O'Ryan leaned in and whispered in Oki's ear, "When she's not in school, Mrs. Pearlman works in one of those dress-em-up theme restaurants!"

"No way! Was she your waitress or something?" Oki asked, picturing Mrs. P. wearing roller skates, a fifties costume, and serving up a giant pickle-covered burger with a large side of fries.

"No, nothing like that," O'Ryan said. "But Reese and I saw her at "Hey, Betty" wearing this spangly dress with high gloves and everything. So, I mean, why else would she be wearing something like that?"

Oki thought about this for a moment. "Well, maybe because she's a back-up dancer in an all-girl band or something."

"Maybe!" O'Ryan said. "But that's equally crazy."

"Or, maybe she's one of those people who dresses up and pretends to live in olden times, like they do in Colonial Williamsburg," Oki added. "Except her olden days are the 1920s when ladies wore all those fun flapper fashions."

"Could be. But it's just weird to think that Mrs. P. does anything at *all*—let alone something so bizarro—besides being our teacher, doesn't it?"

"Totally," Oki replied.

"So, I'm sure she'd be really embarrassed if

anyone knew she had a secret life outside school," O'Ryan said. "That's why we've got to keep this secret between us, okay?"

"See these lips of mine?" Oki said,

pointing. "Consider them zipped."

Oki then pretended to zip her lips closed, and just to make sure, she turned an invisible key in the invisible lock, put the tiny key in the pocket of her jumper and patted it closed.

"Good work," O'Ryan replied.

"Thanks," Oki said out of the corner of her mouth.

Secret safe, the girls returned to their language arts homework. And even though Oki was working hard to come up with the right answers, she was working harder to figure out how she could possibly keep Mrs. Pearlman's secret from whomever she would just *have* to tell next!

"Oh boy, oh boy, oh boy!" said Gwen, as she and Reese sat downstairs (while O'Ryan and Oki were upstairs), doing their math assignment. "This is soooooo not happening!"

Reese twirled her pencil, then tapped the eraser against the "not happening fraction" in question. "You know this one, Gwen," she replied. "I *know* you do, 'cause we've studied it before."

Gwen squeezed her eyes shut. "Ummmm…" she said, as if trying to pull the answer from some sunken treasure chest buried deep at sea.

"Ummm…is it ¼?"

"Un-un," Reese replied. "It's ¾."

"Grrr," Gwen growled in frustration.

"Well, you were *sort of* close," Reese said, patting her best friend on the knee. "You were only wrong by one-half."

Gwen opened her eyes and threw her hands in the air. "How do you even *know* that?"

"Well, 'cause ¾ minus ¼ is ²/4, which is the same as ½," Reese replied.

"What?" Gwen practically moaned. "I just don't get it, and I'm *never* going to. Fractions don't make any sense to me. They may as well be in French!"

"Come on, Gwen, you're definitely going to get it," Reese reassured her. "I mean, I got the hang of them, so I'm sure you will, too."

The truth was, learning fractions had come to Reese as easily as playing the violin. She didn't know why her best friend wasn't catching on as quickly.

"Do you think it might help to have a snack?" Reese asked, standing up and heading in the direction of the kitchen. "I mean, I think the brain works better when it's properly fed.

So we've got some chocolate-chip cookies in the kitchen if you want to give it a try."

"No thanks," Gwen replied, staying put and shaking her head.

No thanks?

Gwen was turning down chocolate-chip cookies—one of her all-time favorite treats (in the cookie family at least)!

This was serious!

"What's the deal?" Reese asked, realizing something must be seriously askew.

"I need to get a good grade on our math test on Thursday," Gwen continued, more serious than Reese had imagined she could be.

"Of *course* you want to do well," Reese, responded. "I understand that."

"No," replied Gwen, "you don't understand. I *need* to do well."

"What do you mean?" Reese asked.

"If I don't," Gwen said, "my mom says I can't go to our next Groovy Girls sleepover this weekend."

A Groovy Girl sleepover *without* Gwen?

Impossible!

Which is why Reese made up her mind right then and there that there was *no way* she was going to let that happen.

Chapter 3

Whatcha Gonna Do?

"One last thing," Mrs. Pearlman said to the class the next day before lunch.

"Think there's any chance she'll tell us she's canceling tomorrow's math test?" Gwen whispered to Reese.

"Ummmm," Reese whispered back, "don't think so."

"Next week we're going to be having a Think-About-What-You're-Going-to-Be-When-You-Grow-Up day," Mrs. P. announced.

"I know what I'm going to be already," Oki shouted. "I'm gonna be taller!"

"No doubt," Mrs. P. said with a laugh. "But this day is to encourage you to imagine what you'd like to do when you grow up based on what you're good at and what comes easily to you."

"You mean, like being a doctor or a lawyer or a construction worker?" O'Ryan asked.

"That's right." Mrs. P. nodded. "But I want you to explore as many ideas as possible. There's a world of possibilities out there. Lots of them unexpected."

"Yeah," O'Ryan said in a giggly whisper to Oki, "like Mrs. P. being a wedding singer after hours! Did you ever think of that one?"

Oki put her hand over her mouth to stop a laugh escaping. She *loved* imagining the "possibilities" of Mrs. P.'s secret life!

"Well, what do you mean by "unexpected," Mrs. P.?" asked Reese.

"Good question," Mrs. P. replied. "Let's think about it this way: How many of you have been to a grocery?"

Everyone raised a hand.

"Now tell me, class, how many of you have ever bought a breakfast cereal?"

Again, every hand went up.

"Right," Mrs. P continued, "name one."

Boo Berry! Cap'n Crunch! Wheaties! Cookie Crisp! everyone shouted out at the same time.

"Oh," said Reese, "so it was someone's job to create all those different types of cereal, right?"

"That's part of it, Reese, good thinking," Mrs. P. said. "Someone's job is to say, 'We should make cereal in the shape of little cookies.'"

"Sweet!" said Gwen. "I could be good at that!"

"And," Mrs. P. continued, "it's another person's job to think of the right name for that cereal, too."

Neat! *Who knew?*

"So, like well-prepared trapeze artists, I want you to cast your nets far and wide and use any resources you want," Mrs. P added. "Now off to lunch you go!"

But instead of heading to the caf, Reese, Gwen, O'Ryan, and Oki jumped from their seats and skipped straight to the computers in the back of the room.

"Google 'Cool Jobs,'" said Reese, putting her hands on Gwen's shoulders as she perched in front of the keyboard.

"Hey, you guys coming to lunch?" asked Yvette, who, with Vanessa, poked her head into the girls' classroom after their grade across the hall let out.

"Maybe in a few minutes," Reese replied.

"What are you doing?" Vanessa asked,

approaching the computer. "Cool Jobs?"

"We're casting our nets far and wide," Gwen explained.

"You're talking fancy stockings when you could be eating lunch?" Yvette asked. "You guys okay?"

"We're researching for What-You're-Going-to-Be-When-You-Grow-Up day," Reese replied.

When Gwen hit the SEARCH button on the computer, then clicked through to the "Groovy Girls Jobs" site, a giant list of jobs—everything from cartoon animators to otolaryngologists to zoologists—appeared before them.

"Well, I know what *I'm* going to be," Vanessa said. "I'm going to be a judge."

"I thought you wanted to be a lawyer," Yvette replied.

"Yeah, well I *did* when I was younger. But now I realize being a judge is better since they're the ones who get to tell the lawyers what they can do and when they've been OVERRULED!"

"Yeah," said Oki, thinking back to the way Vanessa always liked to take control of almost any sitch. "I think you'd be good at that."

"I know what I'm going to

be, too," said Yvette.

"Oh, yeah?" said O'Ryan, looking at the computer screen and getting dizzy with all the choices. "What?"

"A professional singer, of course," Yvette replied. "I mean, I just loved performing at our school talent show so much, I knew then and there that's what I wanted to do for the rest of my life."

"The whole rest of your life, really?" asked Gwen.

"It's so cool how you guys have it all figured out already," Reese said.

"When you guys get to be fifth-graders like us next year, you'll probably have a better sense of it, too," Vanessa replied smugly.

"What's that one?" Oki said, pointing to the screen. "Being a 'Nose'?"

Gwen clicked on the hyperlink for the "Nose," and read the description out loud. "The perfume industry seeks people to help them test new fragrances. As a 'nose,' you'll need a perfect sense of smell and must be able to identify and make sense of various scents."

"Wonder if that would be a good job for me?" Gwen asked. "I mean, with my sniffer I can tell you what's cooking in practically any house on my block!"

"Oh, look," said Oki, "here's a listing for a person to be a party planner. Can you imagine actually getting *paid* to throw parties?"

"Yeah, but if you have to work during the party," Vanessa reasoned, "it probably wouldn't be all that much fun."

"Well, this one sounds like it would be fun," laughed Reese. "A taste tester for an ice-cream maker!"

"But," said Vanessa, sticking her pointer finger in the air, "you could only take one little bite and then you'd have to spit it out, because if you didn't, could you imagine how many ice-cream-brain-freezes you'd get every day?"

"Hey, Gwen, type in 'fashion' and see what the net drags in!" Oki said.

When Gwen did as her friend asked, Oki's mouth dropped open at the long list of options that appeared: accessory designer, buyer, boutique owner, color consultant, fashion editor, pattern maker, photographer, stylist, personal shopper and on and on. "Oh, no!" Oki said. "What a terrible idea *that* was!"

"Why?" O'Ryan asked.

"Because now I have *too* many choices!"

"Don't worry, Oki, I still don't have *any* idea what I'm gonna be in the future, either," O'Ryan replied. "I mean, the only thing that I know that comes naturally to me right now—aside from my ability to head a soccer ball—is my fire-engine red hair."

"Yeah, and just like a fire engine," Reese said, "when people see you coming down the street, they'll get out of your way!"

O'Ryan thought about this for a moment. "So *that's* what I should do then!" she said, throwing her hands up in the air.

"What?" Yvette asked.

"Be a fire chief, of course!" O'Ryan said. "And when people call me 'Red,' it'll fit all around."

"My turn!" Reese said.

"Well, I know from studying with you that math comes naturally to you," Gwen said, turning to her best friend. "You're like a g-een-yus with all stuff math-e-matical, so you've got to do something with that, right? Like maybe you could be a code cracker!"

"Or a banker," suggested Vanessa.

"Or a computer geek," Oki added.

"Understanding math *does* give me a bunch of options, I guess," Reese replied thoughtfully. "I bet commanders of space shuttles have to be really good at math, too."

"Yup," said O'Ryan, "'cause if the commander couldn't count backward, how would she know when to blast off?"

"That'd be so cool if you got to fly to the moon," Gwen said.

"Yeah," Reese replied, beginning to realize that this really *could* be a hot idea.

"But don't you think you'd get really lonely all the way up there in space?" asked Yvette.

"Maybe," Reese said.

"Well then I'd go with you," Gwen volunteered. "'Cause I'd like to fly to the moon, too. I'd be your co-pilot! How fun would that be?"

"How fun?" Reese replied excitedly. "So fun, it'd literally be out of this world!"

Satisfied that they'd charted a solid plan for their future, the judge, the singer, the fire chief, the fashion-something-or-other and the two space cadets bounced out of class and headed for Mission Lunch Meal. And although the next day's math test threatened the fate of the slumber party for Gwen, she decided it was far better to focus on the starry future than on whatever tomorrow's fraction problems would bring.

Chapter 4
The Big Test

"**I**'m so jittery, I'm shaking like a Polaroid picture," Gwen said, holding out a trembling hand to show Reese before school the next morning.

"But Gwen," Reese replied, putting her arm around her best friend and trying to get her to stress less. "You studied super-hard for this math test, so I'm sure you'll do fine."

"I know I studied *reallyreallyreally* hard. We

21

worked together, I made flash cards and my mom helped me too, but still..." Gwen said, trailing off and turning to Oki and O'Ryan, who were standing nearby. "Hey, how much did *you* guys study for today's test?"

"Me?" asked O'Ryan. "I stared at the book for a couple of hours at least. I mean, sure, for part of the time I was staring at the TV, too, but I'm good at multi-tasking."

"I studied pretty hard, also," Oki said. "In fact, even my parents got into the fraction action. At dinner, they made me pass them stuff in pieces. They were, like, 'I'd like a quarter slice of bread and a half a pat of butter, please.' And each time I passed them the right amount, they increased the size of my dessert by an eighth!"

"Wow," Gwen nodded, "that's groovin' schoolin'. How 'bout you, Reese?"

Reese looked down. Even though Gwen was her best friend, she was still a little embarrassed to admit *exactly* how little she'd studied for the test.

"She prepped for *maybe* ten minutes," O'Ryan responded for her sister.

"Ten minutes?" Gwen repeated. "That's, like, nothing."

"No kidding!" O'Ryan replied with a shrug. "Reese just gets this stuff, so she doesn't need to study. But she doesn't want to brag about it to make the rest of us feel bad."

"Whatever," Reese said quickly, trying to change the subject. "Anyway, Gwen, I know you're going to do okay today," Reese added. "Just keep saying to yourself, 'I think I can, I think I can.'"

"Yeah," Gwen replied, exhaling loudly, "but *thinking* I can and actually doing it are two different things. And like you already know, if I *don't* do well, I can't come to the sleepover tomorrow night."

"Happy morning, everyone!" Mrs. Pearlman said, walking into class.

"'Morning, Mrs. Pearlman," some of the students responded quietly, not even bothering to call it a "good morning."

"Well, that doesn't sound like the energetic class I usually have," Mrs. P. said, looking around.

"And I wonder if that might have a *fraction* to do with a little test we're supposed to be having today?"

The class remained silent, but that's because Mrs. P. had just said what everybody was thinking.

"Well," added Mrs. P., "the good news is we're going to get the test out of the way first thing, so you don't have to spend the whole day worrying about it."

"That's more like good news/bad news, isn't it?" Oki whispered to O'Ryan, who rolled her eyes in agreement.

"Okay," Mrs. P. said, putting the test papers upside down on each desk. "The test will last for thirty minutes and I'd like everyone to start at exactly the same time. So on the count of three, please turn your tests over and show me what you know!"

One...

Two...

Two and a half...

Two and three-fourths..

Three!

The Groovies turned their papers over and moved through the test little by little, one fraction at a time. Well, everyone, that is, except Reese,

24

who was flying through the problems as if they weren't really problems at all.

"Ten minutes left," Mrs. Pearlman eventually announced.

Reese continued working steadily, and when she was almost finished, she felt a little nudge at her elbow. Glancing up from her paper, she looked to her side and directly into the face of fear.

Gwen was staring at her.

Gwen, whose hands were now in her hair, whose desk was covered in eraser rubbings, whose cheeks had flushed a bright red. Gwen's eyebrows lifted and she mouthed the word "HELP!"

Reese quickly looked around, at first not quite believing what she was seeing—that her best friend in the whole wide world was asking for assistance on the math test. But when she looked back at Gwen, Reese saw that her BFF was now mouthing the word "PLEASE!"

"Five more minutes, everyone," Mrs. Pearlman announced from the front of the room.

Reese could see from Gwen's paper that she'd barely finished—let alone started!—any of the problems on the test.

It was clear that time was of the essence...and that it was running out! Reese looked down at her paper—her clean, almost entirely finished, answer sheet—and didn't know what to do.

On the one hand, she knew sharing her answers was cheating.

On the other, helping out her co-pilot in a time of need *did* seem like the right thing to do. After all, if they were in the space shuttle together, and Gwen forgot how to land the aircraft, Reese would *definitely* pitch in and help out there.

But back to the first hand. This was supposed to test what you knew, not what your neighbor knew, right?

Then again, back to the second hand, it wasn't like Gwen hadn't studied and was trying to get out of work—she just needed a boost.

But what if—what if—they were to get caught?! Gwen would get into horrible trouble!

Was it worth it?

But when Reese heard Gwen whimper, she couldn't take it anymore. She knew if she were in need, Gwen would come through and help her out. So Reese tucked her fist under her chin and moved her elbow in so that Gwen could get a clear view of her paper, while she finished solving the last problems she had left. A few minutes later, Mrs. Pearlman called time. "Okay, everyone. Please put your pencils down and pass your papers to the front of the room."

MATH TEST

$$\frac{3}{4} - \frac{1}{2} = \boxed{\frac{1}{4}}$$

$$\frac{1}{2} - \frac{1}{8} = \boxed{}$$

When Reese turned to collect the tests of those nearest her, Gwen nodded and smiled. "Thanks," she mouthed to Reese.

Reese pressed her lips together in a half smile. She was glad that she had helped her friend, but was gladder still that the test—and the cheating—was all over.

When the girls lined up for lunch later that morning, Gwen grabbed Reese's hand, swinging it back and forth.

"I'm really lucky to have a best friend and co-pilot like you," Gwen said. "I never could have flown solo on that flight without you."

"Don't mention it," Reese said, shaking her head, hoping, of course, that Gwen would actually *never* mention it again. Wouldn't ask Reese to let her cheat ever again and wouldn't remind her of how she had gone from feeling proud of herself one minute for how she had been doing on the math test to feeling very icky about what she had just let happen in a *fraction* of a second.

Chapter 5

Searching for the Right Answer

"What are you *doing* down there?" Reese asked O'Ryan later that night when she walked into their shared bedroom and found her twin creep on the ground.

"I'm searching," O'Ryan replied as she continued to creep on her hands and knees, lifting the bedspread on Reese's bed and peeking underneath.

"Well, if you're searching for a missing sock, Mom said to forget about it—the dryer eats those!"

"No," O'Ryan replied standing up, "'search' is one of the physical fitness tests you have to take to become a firefighter. You have to crawl on your hands and knees through a long tunnel maze that's only three feet tall."

"That doesn't sound like a test, that sounds more like something for preschoolers at gymboree," said Reese.

"Not when you do it with a really heavy pack on your back," O'Ryan explained. "If I want to be a fire chief when I grow up, I need to be a regular firefighter first. And to be a regular firefighter, I have to pass a physical fitness test."

"Well, you're good at soccer and physical

fitness stuff. And you always score well on the Presidential Physical Fitness thingy in gym class."

"I *know*," replied O'Ryan, "but this isn't

just like the long jump or the hundred-yard dash. You've got to master a 'hose drag,' a 'ladder raise,' and a 'forcible entry.'"

"What's a forcible entry?" Reese asked, sitting down at her desk.

"I'll show you," O'Ryan replied. "Watch." She then walked out of the bedroom and closed the door behind her. "Okay, so when a firefighter is trying to rescue somebody," O'Ryan yelled from the hallway, "sometimes they can't get to that person because a door is locked or jammed. So they have to do this." Backing down the hall and giving herself some running room, O'Ryan jogged toward

the bedroom door and hurled herself against it with all her weight.

Unfortunately, the door stayed shut, but O'Ryan herself *forcibly* slid to the ground.

Hearing the loud thud, the girls' little puppy, Sleepless, started barking wildly and came running upstairs. Reese opened the door from the inside to find her twin in a heap on the floor.

"O'Ryan," Reese said, bending down to give her sister a hand up, "I've heard of stop, drop, and roll, but that was ridiculous. You okay?"

"Uh," O'Ryan said, rubbing her sore shoulder with one hand and patting the puppy, who was now licking her face, with the other. "Maybe I should become a veterinarian instead."

"Problem is," Reese responded, as the girls walked back into their room, "to become a vet, you have to study a ton and take all sorts of tests. And *then*, you wind up having to give puppies their shots!"

"Oh, *man*," O'Ryan replied, flopping on her bed. "This just isn't my day. After that math mess this morning, I'm so over this whole test-taking business. Gwen seemed pretty relaxed about it during lunch, though. Guess all that studying she did really must have paid off, huh?"

"Uh-huh," Reese nodded a little nervously in response.

Reese had been doing her best to put all thoughts of the math test (and the whole cheating business) aside—and she'd been doing pretty well.

Sure, she could barely eat her lunch, had a headache during music class and, for the life of her, couldn't manage to field one ball kicked to her during soccer practice—but aside from that, she was doing just great.

"So, um, here's a random question for you," Reese said.

"Oh, good, I'm a whiz at random stuff!" O'Ryan replied.

"Do you think it's ever okay to cheat on a test?" Reese asked.

"Well, I wouldn't say no if someone else wanted

to take the forcible entry part of the firefighter exam for me," O'Ryan laughed, rubbing her bruised arm.

"So you *do* think it's okay, then?" Reese pressed.

"It depends. Do you get away with it or not?" O'Ryan asked, cocking her head to the side.

"Let's say you do," Reese responded. "Is it okay then?"

O'Ryan tapped her finger to her lips and thought about it for a moment.

Is it ever okay to cheat?

"Well, that's kind of a hard question," O'Ryan admitted. "I mean, getting away with it is better than *not* getting away with it. I know that. But if it's ever okay—that's kinda different. You know who would know for sure, though? Vanessa! She's planning to be a judge after all, so we should ask her."

"Good call," said Reese, dialing their friend's number.

"Whadd-up?" Vanessa said, when she picked up her cell phone.

"Hey *Your Honor*, it's Reese."

"And O'Ryan," O'Ryan added, picking up the second extension in the bedroom.

(When the twins' parents let the girls get a phone line in their room, each girl had different ideas about which phone they should buy. And to avoid an all-out battle, the McCloud's had decided it was just easier to let each girl have her own phone.)

"Hello, McCloud twins, what's going on?" Vanessa asked.

"We have a question for you," O'Ryan said.

"Fire away, Chief!"

O'Ryan looked at Reese and nodded, signaling that she should ask Vanessa since it really was *her* question. Reese hesitated for a moment, then very quickly said: "So, O'Ryan and I were just chit-chatting about a few things, and we were wondering—is it ever okay to cheat?"

Vanessa responded just as quickly. "No way. It's *never* okay to cheat. 'Cause winners never cheat and cheaters never win."

"Well, I don't think that's *always* true," Reese said. "I mean, after all, sometimes when people cheat, they get away with it, and then they *do* win."

"Yeah, but it's like the long arm of the law," Vanessa replied.

"What?" asked O'Ryan.

"Even if you don't get caught right away, the cheat always catches up with you one way or another."

"What do you mean by that?" Reese asked a bit nervously.

"Well," Vanessa replied, "cheating is like a two-part crime. I mean, first of all, the cheater loses out on the experience."

"Keep talking," Reese said. "*How* does she lose out?"

"Well, if the cheater just skates through, chances are she never learns how to do the thing right. Like if you copy someone else's homework, you might never understand how to do it yourself. And the second part of the problem is that the cheater—and the person who lets her cheat—is messing with everyone who did the thing fairly."

"Oh," said Reese, "I hadn't really thought about how cheating affected everyone else. You make a convincing argument, Judge Vanessa."

"Of course I make a convincing argument," Vanessa replied. "After all, arguing is one of the things I do best!"

"That's true," O'Ryan replied, "which is no lie at all."

When the girls hung up their phones, Reese sat at her desk, and her head started filling with questions about how to handle the fact that she'd helped Gwen cheat that morning, which made her a cheater, too:

Should she admit to what happened?

Should she live with the secret?

Should she tell on Gwen?

Should she only confess that she'd let someone cheat off her—without naming any name, like, um, Gwen's?

These were questions that Reese needed to puzzle through. She was sure she'd figure it out eventually, but she didn't have the answer quite yet.

Meanwhile, O'Ryan had gone back to working on her firefighter's "search" technique.

"Right on!" O'Ryan shouted a moment later. "I *knew* fire chief was going to be the right job for me. Look what I found?" she said, crawling out from underneath her bed. "I just searched and rescued this feather boa!"

O'Ryan draped the bright feathery scarf around her sister's neck. "Think I should give this to Mrs. Pearlman?" she asked with a twinkle in her eye. "After all, it might make a good accessory for her to wear to her second job as a 'ta-da! girl' on a TV game show!"

Just the thought of their teacher as a game show sidekick was enough to make both girls stop, drop, and roll with laughter! And for that moment, at least, Reese felt a little relief from all the burning questions that were raging within her.

Chapter 6

Score!

"Gwen—" Mrs. Pearlman said, looking her in the eye the next morning as she handed back the math tests. "Great job!"

Gwen blinked as if not quite believing her ears. And then, when she looked down at the grade on her paper, she blinked again, not entirely sure she could trust her eyes, either!

48/50

"I got forty-eight out of fifty questions right?"

Gwen asked, and Mrs. P. nodded.

She had *never* done so well on a math test. It hadn't even occurred to her that she *could* get such a high score!

"This page is going to go right up on the refrigerator," Gwen said joyously. "Maybe even in a frame! Oh, man, my mom's going to be so happy!" Turning to Reese, Gwen added, "Mom will definitely let me go to our slumber party now. She'll probably even drop me off early and let me stay late!"

"That's supreme, Gwen," Reese replied, catching the excitement of her best friend. "I'm so happy for you!"

"I totally scored!" Gwen beamed.

Yeah, thought Reese, *Gwen: 1, Vanessa: 0*

The judge sure got it wrong on this one, Reese couldn't help thinking, as she thought back on what Vanessa had said last night on the phone.

That whole business about winners never cheating and cheaters never winning? Well, Gwen had cheated—and gotten away with it. She had won.

"How funny! Would you look at this?"

Mrs. Pearlman said, when she circled back to give Reese her test paper. "You girls got *exactly* the same grade on the test. In *fact*, you even got the same two answers wrong!"

Reese quickly bit her lip when Mrs. Pearlman said that, immediately feeling as if she'd just tripped.

But Gwen, still too pleased to consider how suspicious this might look, exclaimed, "You know what they say, Mrs. P., great minds think alike."

"So I've heard," Mrs. P. responded.

"In fact," Gwen continued happily, "Reese and I think so much alike, we're even going to do the same thing when we grow up!"

"We're going to be pilots, she means," Reese explained quickly. "Co-pilots on the space shuttle."

"And you know what the *best* part about it is?" Gwen added.

"What's that?" Mrs. Pearlman asked.

"When your best friend is your co-pilot, you know you'll always have someone there to help you out!"

"That's true," Mrs. P. replied.

"Like if one of us gets tired," Gwen continued, "the other one can fly the shuttle while she takes a nap. And if one of us gets hungry, that girl could go eat a burrito while the other one holds onto the wheel. Or if one of us has to go to the space potty…well, you know."

But as Gwen listed all of the great things about having a trusty co-pilot, Reese looked down again at her test, and Vanessa's words suddenly came back to her.

If the cheater just skates through, chances are she never learns how to do the thing right.

What if now, so jazzed by the way things had turned out on the math test, Gwen planned to rely on Reese to fly their spacecraft on her own?

Reese would *never* be able to leave the flight deck!

Though Reese had always been willing to help out her best friend and co-pilot, she suddenly realized if Gwen didn't master things on her own, the great space adventure they had hoped to have together in the future would actually become *Mission Impossible*!

Chapter 7

Excused Lateness

"**W**here in the world's Gwen?" asked Reese, looking at the kitchen clock that night. "I mean, I *knew* she'd be late, but it's officially later than late now!"

The rest of the Groovies had arrived at the McCloud's more than an hour earlier for their sleepover. And the girls had finally decided they could no longer wait to start making their red 'n' delicious apple-cherry-raspberry pie.

They'd decided to make this sleepover pie for two reasons:

1. They only had red fruit in the fridge.

2. O'Ryan wanted practice making a pie to match her fire-engine-red fire chief's helmet.

"Gwen's always late, Reese." O'Ryan laughed. "You know that. Tell us something we don't already know!"

"Well, sure," Reese replied, "but tonight's different."

Gwen had been looking forward to this slumber party all week. And if ever there was a time for Gwen to arrive early, you'd've thought it would have been to *this* party *this* evening!

"Maybe her mom took her to buy new party PJs," Oki suggested, "to celebrate how well she did on her math test."

"What math test, and please pass the peeler," head chef Yvette said, as she washed the apples in the sink.

"On fractions. We got it back this morning,"

O'Ryan replied, taking the peeler from the drawer and handing it to Yvette. "Gwen was all nervous about it ahead of time."

"She was? And she did really well on it?" asked chief crumble topping-maker Vanessa.

"Gwen's a smart girl," Reese replied, feeling the need to protect her friend.

"No one's saying she isn't," responded Vanessa.

"Well, she must have really gotten the hang of those fractions because she totally rocked on that test," Oki replied, plucking a raspberry from its carton and popping it in her mouth.

"Yeah, she even did as well as Miss Smarty Skirt over here," O'Ryan added, cocking her head toward Reese. "Forty-eight out of fifty."

"Wow, that's great!" Yvette said. "And you guys even got the same score?"

"Uh, yeah," Reese replied, burying her head in the fridge to look for some butter to hold the crumble together.

The cold air from the fridge felt

good on Reese's reddening cheeks.

Ever since that morning, when the girls had gotten their tests back, Reese had been trying to figure out a way to make things right, but so far she'd come up empty.

"I'm here!" Gwen shouted, knocking on the screen door of the kitchen, then letting herself in.

"You're so late, Gwen, we thought you might have taken the space shuttle to Mars," Vanessa replied.

"With Gwen, it would have been to the Milky Way!" O'Ryan laughed.

Gwen looked down at her watch. "Well, the party was called for 7 P.M., and it's 8:15 now, so that means I'm an hour and a quarter late, which is the same thing as being 1.25 hours tardy!"

Huh? Her answer made Reese take notice.

But the other girls were far too busy washing, chopping and pitting their red fruit to pay much attention to what Gwen had said—or to wonder *why* she was later than late that night.

"Hey, please pass the red food dye!" shouted Oki.

"Why do you need food dye?" Vanessa asked.

"Because when you peel these apples, they don't look red enough anymore. And the redder the better, right?"

"What are you guys making?" Gwen asked.

"An apple-cherry-raspberry pie with a crumble topping," Yvette responded.

"Well, let me help!" Gwen said.

"Okay," replied O'Ryan. "We still need to add ³/₄ cup of sugar, but I can't seem to find the right measuring cup."

"Then you can just use the ¹/₂ cup and ¹/₄ cup measurements," Gwen nodded. "Because when you add them together you get ³/₄ cup."

"Very cool! Thank you, fraction queen," O'Ryan replied with a small bow.

"Anytime," Gwen curtsied back.

Huh? Reese thought again. She looked at Gwen and raised her eyebrows. Gwen motioned back with her index finger, signaling Reese to come over to her.

"Do you want to know why I was *really* late tonight?" Gwen said in a low voice, when she and Reese moved to a corner of the kitchen, so the other girls wouldn't hear.

"Of course I want to know! I was getting worried," Reese replied, now packing brown sugar into a measuring cup.

"I was with Mrs. Pearlman."

"You were *what*?" Reese practically shouted, thinking she hadn't heard Gwen right.

"Shhhhh!" Gwen replied.

"Why?" Reese asked.

"Well, even though I *had* been really happy with my math test grade this morning, the more I thought about it, the more it started bothering me. See, I just didn't feel right about taking a grade I didn't earn," Gwen said.

"No?" Reese asked.

"Then I realized I was going to be in even more trouble on the next math test because I still don't know the basic stuff," Gwen continued.

"Oh?" Reese said.

"And *then* I realized I hadn't been fair to you, either," Gwen said, pushing the bangs off her forehead. "So, at the end of the day, when I told you to go ahead because I'd forgotten my book in our room, I actually stayed to talk to Mrs. P. and I told her I had cheated."

"You did? Was she mad? Is...is she going to fail us both?" Reese gulped, wondering how this option was really going to be "fair" to her.

"First of all," Gwen replied, taking her pal's hand and trying to reassure her. "I didn't tell Mrs. P. that it was you who helped me cheat."

"You didn't?" Reese asked, her stomach flipping back into the position it was in a minute earlier.

"Of course I wouldn't tell on my BFF like that!" Gwen confirmed. "But she knew it was you, anyway."

"She did??? You mean because we're best friends and our desks are right next to each other?" Reese asked, accidentally knocking the box of brown sugar off the counter in her distress.

"Because," Gwen replied, bending down to pick up the box, "not only did we get the exact same grade, and the exact same two answers wrong, we answered them incorrectly in exactly the same way, too!"

"D'oh!" Reese exclaimed. "I didn't even realize that." She pushed the spilled sugar into a big lump on the floor.

"Yeah, so I told Mrs. P. that I really *had* studied a lot for the test—she could even call my mom and check with her—but that I just never quite got the hang of the material."

"*Did* she call your mom?" Reese asked, wondering if she, too, could expect a phone call home.

"We called her together." Gwen nodded. "I told my mom what happened, and then Mrs. P. told her she gave me a lot of credit for coming forward on my own and realizing that what I had done was wrong. *And then* she said she had a deal to offer me."

"What was it?"

"Well, she said she'd give me some extra tutoring one-on-one. And that she'd even be happy to do it later today after school."

"Whoa," Reese replied. "That *was* really groovy of her."

"I know!" Gwen said. "And talking about groovy, you should see her house!"

"Her house?!" Reese asked.

"Yup, that's where we went, so *that's* where I was," Gwen replied.

"Well, I'm glad for you, Gwen," Reese replied to her smiling friend, "but where do you think that leaves me? I mean, now she knows I'm a cheater, too!"

"Um," Gwen answered, scratching her head, "that's a good question! But I don't think you have to worry about it too much. I mean, look how well things worked out for me!"

"Hey, whatever you guys are whispering about, it can't be as important as this pie," Yvette said, "and besides, we need Gwen's help."

"Yeah, right now we need you to measure out the amount we need for the crumble topping," O'Ryan added.

"It's the last thing we have to do before we put the fruit in the pie," Yvette said.

"I'm here to serve," Gwen saluted, expertly mixing fractional amounts of cinnamon and sugar.

"Okay, now fill 'er up!" Yvette instructed Oki. After Oki scooped the fruit mixture into the pie crust, she smoothed it out with a spoon. Then she nodded at Gwen, who was given the honor of spreading the crumble on top.

"I can't believe we have to wait for fifty minutes before we can eat this pie!" Gwen said. "'Cause I can't wait to cut it in half and then in quarters and then in eighths and—"

"And then we're not going to let you cut it anymore 'cause we're going to want to eat it

already!" Vanessa said, laughing.

But even though Reese was happy to know there was pie on the way—and pleased her co-pilot now knew how to divide it up into perfect fractions—she wasn't quite as delighted as she wanted to be.

After all, she still had a bad taste in her mouth—and had no idea what type of punishment she might be asked to swallow come Monday morning.

Chapter 8

To Do-Be Do-Be Doo!

"Excuse me, Mrs. P.?" Reese said, poking her head into the empty classroom before school started Monday morning. "Can I talk to you a sec?"

"Sure, come on in, Reese," Mrs. P. replied. "Hey, where's your career-day costume?"

"I have it in my bag, but I needed to tell you something before I change." Reese looked down, still unsure exactly what she was going to say.

"Well...okay, the thing is...I know you know I let Gwen copy my math test last Thursday...and the thing is, I didn't really want her to. But she's my best friend and all, so I didn't really see how I couldn't let her. Anyway, I wanted you to know how bad I've been feeling about the whole thing."

Mrs. P. nodded. "Thank you for letting me know. I think it was brave of you to tell me that."

"I know letting Gwen copy my answers on that test was wrong," Reese added. "And because she cheated off me, that kind of makes me a cheater, too." Reese took a deep breath, then continued. "So I understand if you need to punish me."

"Well," Mrs. P. said, "as I think you know, I don't like to punish anyone—but I will do it if I think it'll help them learn a lesson."

Reese nodded, and tried to prepare herself for whatever punishment was to come.

"But," Mrs. P. continued, "in this case, I think you've already learned a very valuable lesson. You realize that cheating is wrong. You feel bad that you participated in it, and I assume you're not going to do it again. Is that right?"

"No way!" Reese replied. "I mean, right! I'll never do it again, and I'm going to tell my mom about it, just to keep her in the loop, too."

"I think that's an excellent idea," Mrs. P. said with a smile. "And after that, why don't we just close the book on this one, and it'll be like we're starting fresh with a new chapter, okay?"

When Reese realized that Mrs. P. was not only *not* going to punish her, but also believed in her, too, it felt as if a knot in her stomach had come undone.

"Now if you'll excuse me, Reese," Mrs. Pearlman continued, standing up, "I have to go to the teachers' lounge before class starts."

As Mrs. P. walked out of the room, Oki and O'Ryan, both dressed in their think-about-what-you're-going-to-be-day costumes, entered.

"Oki, I just noticed something," O'Ryan said to her best friend. "You're wearing two different shoes!"

"I know! Isn't it just hip to the jive?" Oki replied, pointing to her mismatched tootsies. "I did it on purpose."

"You did? Why? Are you trying to be funny?"

"No!" Oki replied, shaking her head and putting her hands on her hips. "I'm going to be a footwear designer!"

"Aha!" O'Ryan replied, pushing her firefighter's helmet up and out of her eyes. "I mean, I knew you wanted to be something fashiony. Maybe you'll even be able to design groovier boots for me to wear as part of my firefighter's uniform."

Oki considered the problem. "Well, I'm thinking with all the ladders you'll be climbing, they shouldn't be high-heeled boots."

Gwen walked in a moment later wearing some pretty cool booties herself. "Look!" she said to O'Ryan, "I got these moon boots at your mom's store!"

Gwen had done a great job with her space shuttle co-pilot outfit, with its special "anti-gravity" jumpsuit and fishbowl helmet. But Oki was most excited about those boots!

"See that?" Oki said. "The shoes make the career!"

"Hey, look over there! I spy my co-pilot," Gwen said, approaching Reese.

While Reese had yet to change into her career-day outfit, she *was* wearing something that Gwen was super-pleased to see.

A Super Giant Smile!

"Good Morning, Dimples," giggled Gwen.

"It sure *is* a good morning," Reese replied. Then, she whispered, "I just talked to Mrs. P."

"Yeah?" Gwen replied.

"And after I told her how bad I felt and what a huge mistake I knew I made, she made me feel much better about things!"

"Eggs-cellent," Gwen replied. "She's a pretty classy lady."

And then, almost exactly on cue, Mrs. Pearlman walked in looking very classy indeed...

"Shazaam!" O'Ryan exclaimed, turning to Oki, "I can't believe it. That's the spangly dress Reese and I saw on Mrs. P. at "Hey, Betty!" Look, it all shakes around when she moves!"

"And would you just check out her shoes!" Oki replied, her mouth agape. "They're gorgeous!"

Sure enough, Mrs. P. was wearing a very special pair of patent leather T-strap high heels.

"Mrs. P.?" Oki said. "As a future fashion designer, I have to tell you I *adore* the clothes, but you're supposed to be our fourth-grade teacher, not—"

"A wedding singer!" O'Ryan chimed in.

"Or a disco queen!" Oki added.

"Or a waitress at a dress-'em-up restaurant!"

"Or an extra in a movie about the 1920s!"

"Oh, I see, is that everything you think I could possibly be dressed as?" Mrs. P. asked. "Well, you already know that I'm a teacher, but you might not know that your teacher has a good number of hobbies, too!"

Hitting the PLAY button on the tape recorder on her desk, Mrs. P. began to nod her head in synch with the pulsing, plucky beat. "This is the music of the tango," she explained, as she began to slide and glide her body across the front of the room, dancing with an imaginary partner.

Before long, Mrs. P. grabbed Reese's hand and invited her to be her real dance partner. The duo dipped their way around the room.

And though everyone in the class started laughing, the more they watched, the more they wanted to join in, too!

"When I was in fourth grade," Mrs. Pearlman said, "at first, I thought I wanted to be a professional tango dancer. But then I kept coming up with other things I wanted to be, too, like an archery champion! A stained glass window maker!

I even thought about writing a new dictionary!"

"With the way I spell," O'Ryan said, "I think I could come up with a new dictionary, too!"

"But it never really occurred to me that I'd become a teacher," she said. "And yet here I am, and I love what I do. Even though I still love to tango as a hobby."

"That's so supreme!" Gwen replied.

"And fun!" Oki exclaimed.

"It *is* fun," Mrs. P. nodded. "So just know, whatever you choose to do later, you should always keep doing other things that tickle you, too!"

As Mrs. P. was explaining this, she started to pair up dance partners around the room.

And as she handed off Reese to her new partner, Gwen, Reese's smile grew even larger, as she realized that it just might be possible to pursue the two things she wanted to do most.

"Hey!" Gwen said to her best friend forever. "So what happened to the rest of your co-pilot costume?"

"Well, I've decided that I want to be a part-time space shuttle pilot and a part-time teacher, too," Reese replied.

"Really?" Gwen asked, trying to scratch her head, but forgetting there was a helmet in the way.

"Yeah, I mean, if the whole world is open to me, why not try to get to the moon while teaching others how to reach for the stars?"

"Well, when you put it that way, it *does* sound pretty good," Gwen replied, "even if I would *never* want to be a teacher myself. I mean, the last thing I want to do when I'm older is to have to get to class on time!"

When the song ended, everyone went back to their seats, ready to talk about what they hoped to become in the future.

And as Gwen reached her desk with Reese, she said, "Wonder what a Groovy Girls slumber party would be like on another planet?"

Reese smiled. "I already know the answer to that one!" she replied.

"You do?" Gwen asked.

"Of course. It would be out of this world!"

The girls both laughed, knowing for certain that whatever they did down the road, it'd be remarkable. And as long as they were together, it'd also be a real BLAST!

Groovy Girls™

sleepover handbook

How to Make Your Very Own JOURNAL

7

GROWING UP GROOVY: Lots of Fun and Games

What to Do When YOUR FRIEND WANTS TO CHEAT OFF YOU

SWEET Sleepover PIE

Contents

Text by Suzanne Francis
Illustrations by Yancey Labat and Kurt Marquart

A Groovy Greeting

HEY THERE, GROOVY GIRL!

GWEN: It's just me and my co-pilot coming at you—

REESE: Wait! Ten, 9, 8, 7, 654321! Blastoff!

GWEN: What was that for?

REESE: I was just giving us a countdown before we started chatting about the groov-alicious stuff in this handbook.

GWEN: Gotcha. Now, you and your buds can have fun with all kinds of ways to grow up groovy when you throw a "Sky's the Limit" slumber party (see pages 4–6). You'll get to dress up, use your imagination…

REESE: And even stick Post-its on your head!

GWEN: That game's my fave!

REESE: Oh! And wait till you check out the crazy careers on pages 8 and 9! You won't believe some of the really kooky jobs out there. Like ice cream developer!

GWEN: Oooh! Actually, just the thought of it is making me kinda hungry…

REESE: Me too! So, if you're ready for a serious snack, check out our groov–alicious Sleepover Pie (see pages 12–13).

GWEN: And you can practice your fractions at the same time. It really works. There's no yummier way to study math!

REESE: I think we'd better steer this ship over to the kitchen for a landing!

GWEN: Okay! Just remember, fellow Groovy Girl, to dream big and always reach for the stars.

REESE: And maybe we'll see you in outer space one day!

Love, Reese and Gwen

Sky's the Limit
✷ Sleepover

What could be more fun than
dreaming about the future with your
best friends? Throw a Sky's the Limit slumber
party and watch everybody's imagination
shoot through the roof! Get the action started
with some super-fun games like:

Pass the Prop!

✳ Flex your creative "what-I-can-be-when-I-grow-up" muscles
and see what you come up with! First, write down a bunch
of career ideas on little pieces of paper. Fold them up and
toss them into a bag or hat. Then collect a bunch of different
props (see the examples below for ideas) and put them into
another bag or hat.

✳ Sit in a circle with your friends. Pass the two bags around
and have each girl pick one prop and one profession
without looking at them first. Then take turns coming
up with a creative way to use the prop together with the
career you've "chosen." Be inventive! Here are some ideas
to get you started:

The prop is a scarf: If you choose Oki's favorite
career (fashion, of course!), you might wrap the
scarf around your waist to make a super-mini
skirt, or tie it around your hair for a flowing
headband. Or maybe the career you pick is
Modern Dancer. In that case, you could wave
the scarf around while performing. Don't be
afraid to stand up and get into it!

The prop is aluminum foil: If you pick Hair Stylist, you might fold the foil into strips to put into your customer's hair to give her highlights. Or maybe you're a Jewelry Designer, and you twist some of the foil into a groovy necklace. If you're a Journalist, you can shape the foil into a microphone and use it to interview a famous athlete.

The prop is a plateful of cookies wrapped in colorful cellophane: If your career is Actor in a TV Commercial, you might get up and perform with the cellophane. Maybe you hold it upside down while talking about how amazing the cellophane is. Or if the job you choose is Spy, those cookies might contain a hidden camera for your secret mission!

The prop is glittery, sparkling gloss: If your profession is Singer, maybe you get ready for a big performance by putting the gloss in your hair to highlight your ponytail, or by dabbing it onto your cheekbones to call attention to your pretty face. If you're a Nose, maybe you're sniffing the gloss to say whether you think the flavor (say, it's cinnamon) will be a hit with shoppers—or not.

The prop is a shopping bag: If you're a Personal Shopper, you might be returning from a shopping spree. Or, if you picked Wardrobe Costumer, the bag might be full of alien costumes for a hot new movie, *Rockin' Out in Outer Space.*

I ♥ my personal shopper

What Am I?

❋ Part of the fun of imagining what you'll be when you grow up is thinking about what you'll be wearing, right? Play this game of charades dressed in "career" costumes to see what everyone might look like in the future! The more possibilities an outfit has, the more fun it will be.

❋ If you throw on your cute denim overalls, what might you be? A construction worker or a house-painter? How about an artist, like a sculptor? If your friend comes dressed in a lab coat, is she a dentist? Maybe she's a scientist who does research in a lab, or perhaps she's a doctor. Or even a beautician. Get the idea? Another friend might come wearing a sweat suit. Is she a personal trainer? A gym (or yoga) teacher? An Olympic gymnast? Let your imagination take off. The possibilities are limitless.

Stuck on You

You gotta ask the right questions to figure out who you are in this fun game. First, think of as many careers as you can and write each one down on its own Post-it note. Fold the Post-its and toss them into a hat. Now have everyone pick one—without peeking! When it's your turn, have a pal stick the sticky onto your forehead (so you can't see it but everyone else can). You should feel pretty clueless right about now! Ask your friends questions like:

❋ "Does my job make me famous?"
❋ "Do I get to travel a lot?"
❋ "Am I the boss?"

How many questions does it take until you've figured out what career is *stuck* on you?

To Cheat or Not to Cheat
and ACTIVITY JUGGLING ACT

Is your bud asking you to let her cheat off you? Got more after-school stuff to do than you have time to do it in? Kiss those questions good-bye by checking out these smart solutions.

Friends and Cheating

My best friend wants me to let her copy off our spelling test. I'm afraid if I don't let her, she'll stop being my friend. What should I do?

It sounds like you're going through the same sitch Reese did when Gwen wanted to copy her math answers during their fractions test. Being a friend means being supportive, so it makes sense that you want to help your BFF out. Even though helping her cheat might get her a passing grade this time—and even if helping her weren't cheating—that kind of help definitely won't work for her in the long run. The best help you can give her is *before* the test. Offer to study with her or encourage her to ask your teacher for extra after-school help. Then, when she gets a passing grade on her own, you can *both* celebrate!

Busy Girl Blues

I have tons of hobbies and after-school activities every day of the week. But I don't have enough time! How am I ever going to decide what I want to be? And how can I fit it all in?

It's groovy that you have so many interests. Figuring it all out is half the fun, so enjoy—you're doing exactly what you should be doing! But remember, busy girl, there are only 24 hours in a day. You still need time to unwind, relax, sleep, and spend with family and friends! Too many activities can have the *opposite* effect of being engaging: they can actually stress you out.

7

You Do WHAT?
Groovy Career Ideas

Having fun eating ice cream might not sound like a real job. But believe it or not, people actually get paid to do it! Check out these fun and funky careers—and who knows? Maybe you'll find one that's just groovy enough for you!

Ice Cream Flavor Developer

Before a new flavor of ice cream hits the store shelves, it has to pass the ice cream developer's tests. As an ice cream tester, you try out new ice cream ideas, invent your own flavors, and probably get lots of brain freezes (not to mention cold tongues). How about: "Chocolate-y Chunk 'n' Pizza!" Yummy or nasty? If you were an ice cream flavor developer, it'd be your job to decide!

Animal Trainer

How do movie directors get animals to do tricks for their flicks? Will a dog just start playing basketball, if you give him the ball and a pair of sneakers? Not likely! If you put a chimp in tap shoes and stick him in front of a camera, will he start dancing? Uh, don't think so! That is, not unless you have an animal trainer on hand. Animal trainers know how to work with animals to get them to do whatever crazy antics they've got to do. Say, "Cheese," Fido!

Singing Messenger

If you were a singing messenger, you'd dress up in costume and deliver a message—say, a birthday greeting—by performing it. You might be asked to dress up as a giant birthday cake on roller skates and sing "Happy Birthday" at the top of your lungs to the lucky birthday girl. It's like being a living greeting card!

Guess What They Do!

Check out these weirdo jobs and try and guess what you'd actually do if each of them were yours to do! Then see how you did.

❀ Puzzle Master

❀ Dinosaur Duster

❀ Doll Doctor

❀ Wrinkle Chaser

❀ Professional Laugher

❀ Potato Chip Fryer

❀ Page Turner

❀ Dog Sniffer

❀ Laughter Therapist

✳ Creates word puzzles for newpapers and magazines.

✳ Dusts dinosaur bones in museums.

✳ Helps dolls in need of a makeover, from a broken arm to a missing eye.

✳ Irons wrinkles from shoes before they hit the shelves.

✳ Laughs on tape for the "laugh track" of TV shows (it's what you hear in the background when watching some funny programs)

✳ Operates the fryer that makes potato chips in a restaurant's kitchen.

✳ Turns the pages of the musical score for a piano player while she's performing.

✳ Smells a doggie's breath to test products like biscuits and pooch toothpaste.

✳ Helps people stress less by using laughter.

Food Stylist

Is that burger ready for its close-up? If you're a food stylist, it's your job to make sure it is! Food stylists make what you eat look great for TV commercials and magazine or Internet ads. On any given day, you might have to search through hundreds of sliced pickles to find the one that's most perfectly rippled. Or you might find yourself carefully arranging sesame seeds on a bun with tweezers and glue. Yuck! If that burger looks a little dry, you might even spritz it with hairspray to make it look juicy. A food stylist knows how to turn a burger—or any other food—into a work of art!

9

Who You Gonna Be?

See how your personality fits with a bunch of careers.

Are you an OBSERVER?

* Do you absorb everything that goes on around you?
* Do you remember details of conversations that make your friends say, "How did you remember that?"

OBSERVERS make great: Writers, Journalists, Photographers, Artists

Are you a NURTURER?

* Do all your friends look to you when they need reassurance?
* Are you the one who shows up with magazines and DVDs when your bud is stuck in bed with a week-long flu?
* Do you volunteer to take care of the classroom pet (turtle, rabbit, gerbil) and bring him home with you during school vacations?

NURTURERS make great: Counselors, Pediatricians, Nannies

Are you a PERFORMER?

* Do you love being on stage in front of an audience?
* Are you always the first to jump onto the dance floor?
* Do you think it'd be awesome to have a portable spotlight that you could take with you anywhere?

PERFORMERS make great: Singers, Actors, Musicians, Dancers, Trapeze Artists

Are you an ATHLETE?

* Do you sign up to play more sports than you can fit into your schedule?
* Are you happiest when you're outside biking, hiking, roller skating, or doing cartwheels across the lawn?

ATHLETES make great: Professional Sports Players, Coaches, Gym Teachers, Personal Trainers

Are you an ADVENTURER?

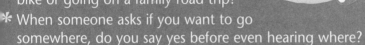

* Do you love to travel to new and exciting places—whether it's discovering a new path on your bike or going on a family road trip?
* When someone asks if you want to go somewhere, do you say yes before even hearing where?
* Are you always up for tasting a funky new food or taking up a new sport or playing a new game?

ADVENTURERS make great: Pilots, Spies, Scuba Divers, Ambassadors

Are you an ORGANIZER?

* When all your friends are trying to figure out what to do on a Friday night, are you always the one with the great ideas?
* Do you plan your slumber parties way in advance, so you have plenty of time to arrange everything the way you want it?
* Do you keep your room so super neat that most of your friends wonder how you do it?

ORGANIZERS make great: Teachers, Principals, Activity Directors, Tour Guides, Party Planners

Are you CREATIVE?

* Do you love coming up with new ideas or new ways to express yourself?
* Do you spend time painting or drawing, daydreaming, writing in your journal, staging a play?
* When your friends are tired of the same old game, do they count on you to come up with a new one?

CREATIVE people make great: Inventors, Chefs, Artists, Photojournalists, Designers, Moviemakers

SLUMBERRIFIC SLEEPOVER PIE

Make and bake this red 'n' delicious apple-cherry-raspberry pie at your next sleepover—just like the Groovies do in *Growing Up Groovy!*

Ingredients:

2 ready-made refrigerated pie crusts (one package should come with 2 crusts)

4 extra-large apples (Granny Smith or Pink Lady are good choices)

3/4 cup fresh raspberries

1/2 cup canned pitted cherries

1 cup sugar

1 tablespoon flour

Utensils: Pie dish, cookie sheet, spoon, fork, butter knife, bowl, paper towels

What You Do:

1. Ask an adult to pre-heat the oven to 375 degrees.

2. Take the ready-made pie crusts out of the fridge to let them get to room temperature.

3. Rinse the raspberries and gently pat them dry with a paper towel.

4. Rinse your apples. Then have an adult peel and slice them. Put them into a bowl.

5. Add the raspberries, cherries, sugar, and flour to the bowl. Mix all the ingredients.

6. Take one of the pie crusts and lay it flat in your pie dish. Use a fork to gently press it down into the dish.

7. Pour the fruit mixture on top of the pie crust.

8. Take the other pie crust and lay it on top of the fruit. Pinch the edges of the top and bottom crusts together to seal them and make a wavy design.

9. Use a butter knife or fork to make slits in the top of the pie so air can come out. If you're feeling artistic, make the slits in a pretty pattern!

10. Bake the pie for about an hour. Let it cool for half an hour. Enjoy!

Add vanilla ice cream or whipped topping onto a warm slice for Sleepover Pie à la mode!

Fractions never tasted so yummy!

FRACTIONS ARE DELISH!

You can master fractions, just like Gwen did, as you cut your pie. Here's how:

1. Make the first cut right down the middle, from top to bottom, to cut your pie in half.

2. Next, cut the pie across, from side to side. (The cuts in your pie will look like a plus sign.) You'll have four even slices. Or four quarters.

3. Now cut the pie diagonally both ways to make an X across the plus sign. Voila! You now have eight even slices. Or eight eighths.

13

Make a Groovy Journal

Keep track of all the groovy things you love to do now—or think you might like to do when you grow up—in your very own make-it-yourself journal.

What You Need:

- Pretty paper (For journal cover, use poster-board or cardboard. For journal pages, use construction or writing paper.)
- Ribbon or yarn
- Glue
- Hole-puncher
- Pencil
- Scissors
- Ruler

What You Do:

1. Pick out some poster-board or cardboard to use for your journal's front and back covers. (It's a good idea to have some extra sheets handy, in case you have to call "do-over!") Choose some paper for your pages. A good size for your journal is 5$\frac{1}{2}$ inches wide by 8$\frac{1}{2}$ inches high. You can use standard sheets (8$\frac{1}{2}$ inches by 11 inches) and cut them in half. A pencil and a ruler will help you measure straight lines before you cut them.

2. After you've cut all the inside pages (ten sheets or more), use your pencil to mark the two holes you'll need on the left side of the journal front and back covers. Measure 1$\frac{1}{2}$ inches from both the top and bottom of the page, and about $\frac{1}{2}$ inch in from the left edge. Make sure your marks line up, so that the holes will too.

3. Punch a hole in each place where you made your pencil marks on the covers. Now punch holes in all the journal pages, too. You can use the covers you already measured as a pattern. Just line one of the punched covers up with the un-punched paper to make your holes. You can punch several sheets at a time, depending on the strength of your hole-puncher.

4. Now it's time to decorate your covers. Get creative! You can glue ribbon, pom-poms, jewels, beads or glitter onto your cover. You can also use wrapping paper or fabric to make a design or collage. Use scraps for shapes or letters.

5. After you've finished designing your cover, cut a nice long piece of yarn or ribbon (about 48 inches long). Lay the yarn or ribbon on top of the journal and thread it through the holes of the cover and pages to hold it all together. Bring each end of the ribbon back up through the opposite hole and tie it in a bow on top. (Don't pull too tight—you'll want to keep the ribbon or yarn loose enough to make it easy to open your journal.)

6. Fold the cover of your journal back, making a crease next to the holes so that you can open it. Continue to crease the pages the same way, so you can flip through your journal like a book.

Grab your favorite pen and start writing!